I0772585

Adalay Sunrise

A Collection of Sonnets By
Stephen Martin Carr

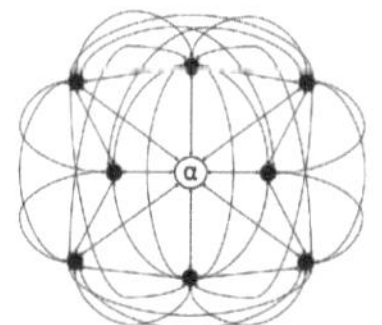

Adalay Sunrise
Copyright © 2022 by Stephen Carr

Cover design by Stephen Martin Carr.
Author Photograph by Brenda L. Carr.
Editing and book formatting by Pen & Pad Publishing.

Printed in the United States of America
ISBN 979-8-9859478-0-9 (pbk)
ISBN 979-8-9859478-1-6 (hcv)

Pradisia Publishing
Fairfax, VA

www.pradisia.com
scarr@pradisia.com
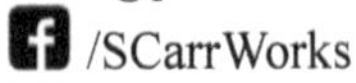 /SCarrWorks
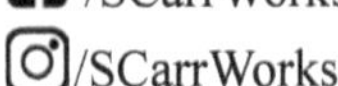/SCarrWorks

For: Elizabeth
Ecstatic Life In Zeitgeist
Amassing Beautiful Eternal True Hope

Introduction on Purpose

The content and purpose of this text is in regard to my conscious awareness of human life and experience of the non-physical, non-material entity called love. This is written for understanding and explicating both my actions and emotions. Performed by delving deep into the intentional and unforeseen consequences of my life, this is the truth and reality that I am now forced to face every day. This knowledge is made to be shared by everyone in order to raise awareness of thought and provide contentment in life. Please read carefully, remembering to keep an open mind and heart.

Peace-Love. All human beings.

Background Information

Stephen was born in the Fall. It seemed that from the beginning his mood was destined to reflect the cold, death and sojourn that is the season. He hurt for all his life; life was an ensuing torture lulled by moments of sweet release. Stephen craved release more than anything. His crave was filled with what he found to be the purest, most innocent and satisfying: love. He craved love most of all. He then found what he sought out to have, and it was everything and more than he could imagine. Love was dizziness, a swirling passion. Fire surged through his veins with every kiss. But Stephen nearly smothered the fire and love did not last. His heart still burned with a flicker. If only the fire could get swirling again, sparks would reignite and passion would blaze again. Stephen spent long nights over many years waiting.

His hope was only met with grief, so he sought out and found a new love. Stephen went about the day with holes in his head. He walked with gaps in perception filled with momentary wonder. He was new and different. His mood was hidden and it didn't seem to affect him. In the middle of Stephen's seeming self-discovery, along came a spider. He was always terrified of spiders, but somehow fell in love. Smooth, sexy, gentle; this was the spider. And the two wove a web tight with one another. Stephen's web was straight with even angles weak at the joints. The spider's web was a circle that twisted and bent inside itself for support. Stephen's web was beautiful but flimsy, ultimately a useless web. The spider's web was functional but for the wrong purpose, ultimately a useless web. In a calculated coup de grâce from a fanciful femme fatale, their delicate webs so carefully woven together tore asunder.

Amidst the dust and rubble of the aftermath, Stephen now sits quietly. He remembers his life's struggle for love, the tender, soft escape. He remembers his favorite childhood hobby. Stephen would take apart the stapler to see how it worked. But he also remembers putting the stapler back together. He now knows that love is not a toy, nor is it for sale; he may not go shopping for love. Stephen hurts no more; he no longer seeks release. Life is unforgiving and there will always be pain, but he knows how to wait. He knows now to truly appreciate those moments when life deals you one fine hand. Stephen is unaffected by his somber mood. He smiles because he has known pain, fear and loss. He smiles because he has known love.

Contents

Patience & Waiting

At the start of this endeavor I spoke of permanency, assuming
Izzy would always be with me.

Future of love in its infinite entirety. Contradictory; we were in
love, but did not love one another properly.

I had nostalgia for the past and always looked to the future, but
no focus on the present or given moment.

Now presently, my status is confused atonement: paradoxical; I
loved her, however I never showed it.

My confusion lies in the discrepancy of the eternal, undeniable
truth that paradox is persistent.

There is both right and wrong in every moment, coexisting and
creating our conscious existence.

We feel most alive when it's the Reaper we see. What I desire the
most is forsaken from me.

The underlying paradox I know in my soul: my love for Izzy was
beyond my capacity to control.

She'll never see how she hurt me. I'll never know the degree my
words damaged her surely.

For this reason remiss, I claim no blame on either of us due to our
childish ignorance.

Not to make excuses, but what do children do with adult pleasures
but be overzealously abusive?

My hands are for her body. Our eyes met, she truly saw me. She in
my arms, I could sleep calmly.

How long will this anticipation increase; before we are together
and this nightmare will cease?

When will our lives and hearts again be at an equivalent rate? In
time, a long time. I will wait.

Sitting

Once upon a time on a midnight dreary, I pondered somber while weak and weary:
I can't think clearly and dreams are nearly scaring me to death. Screaming, "Somebody hear me!"
Breathing is a painful activity. In a cage I rage in captivity. All in all, I'm just a casualty.
This life is happening; this is really happening. But why must it happen so haphazardly?

Can't even pace or mill; must sit still. A way with will. My mind shouts shrill; gives my body a chill.
Not really sick, still my soul feels ill. Sitting on a windowsill, it's sickening reminiscing how love was such a thrill.
My restless mind is racing through time. Another lover? Stuck stubborn; withhold or kill? None other than a soldier's drill.
In sadness I recall I once had this wish, want and will. I'm tired of living with nil. I hope you may learn that forgiving is a skill.

There's a barrier between, it seems love is quite a thin line. Flirting with the time, not noticing a sign.
Is love a crime? Maybe it may be after you steal the time. Surreal to find: only wasted time; lonely wasted mind.
Paradox of mine: if I wait more time, my life may be fine. Slave bound by time; set me free from the bind.
Impossible miracle of the Prime: liars tell the truth upon the shrine, thus when we die any dark lie truly shall shine.

Bound by my brain though I didn't happen to know, so now I wade in the pain with nowhere to go.
Love's what we stole; I know my soul's not whole. Though sitting writing this scroll, I have learned control.

BE

Reality means: none other than nothing; nothing's as it seems. Life is unfair; no care for dreams, but still there are better things.

Like a love letter so intrinsically intriguing, leading lovely eyes to meaning; invisibility to true seeing.

Reality: a feeble fallacy; the simple veil of viewing is a falsity. True passion in both virtue and rude action we see, so please don't disregard both subjective rationality and objective actuality.

Tell the truth indelibly; view truth, the actuality. Calm attention we must pay to the con of the cliché: life will be taken away.

We will die any day by any necessary means, thus I shall lead the way for all ends, true beings. We are not merely means.

Peace-love, all human beings and above all other things, there's something telling me: "We are truly free."

Don't live in suspense; care with common sense and simply let it be. Power in the pen, we write eternity.

Don't fear insecurity or dim uncertainty; always more to what you see. If you get what you give, we live eternally.

If life's not right, you have to change it on your own. I hold to my own so hold close to what is known:

Raw zeitgeist, but that's just life's flow. So go quickly to a slow, to know it's so logical that dreams are possible.

Tolerable and responsible to do justice and remember: the Demon from the deep did keep a hidden agenda.

Seems she decreed: "Your love is a ruse; an Act instead of love. For fools; false facts, feelings, et cetera…"

Time to hold these truths I adorn self-evident: each and every one of you are worthy and were born equivalent.

And endowed rights by the crowned Benevolent. That among these: life, liberty and the pursuit of smiling.

If

If I had known somehow I'd be the bad guy; if I had known
somehow I'd make her cry...
If I had known that now I'd see my love die; if I had owned my
vow; not told a lie...
If I had known our story could be cliché; if I had loaned some love
instead of dismay...
If I had shown the glory, not the disdain; if I had known that now
I'd be so insane...

If I had known somehow I'd feel this shame; if I had known how
to train my brain...
If I had known to simply love without complaint; if I had known
or shown some real restraint...
If I had known somehow that love can create; if I had known that
hate can actually negate...
If I had known never to be petty with picky debate; if I had known
I'd be trapped in my tragic state...

If I had known or had real understanding; if I had ridden the
righteous path to feel love notwithstanding...
If I had known life's prerequisites of peace, prayer and planning;
if I had known that vice can be damning...
If I had known despite what I was told; if I had loathed the sight
of Hell that happened to unfold...
If I had known always to simply say, "I love you;" if I had known
all ways in this life we live through...

I would have given my all, for I am all for you. I didn't have a clue
but now I know this to be true:
If you only knew you are the one who has made me anew. You're
my reason to live and all that I do.

THE DAY

Be patient, stay. I've been waiting for the day to simply say, "Hello
dear, my darling Adalay."
Keep hope deep, she will forever rise. One day I'll swim again in
those vanilla eyes.
It's my fuel to fly high and support this ill addiction. Still I stand
firm like a soldier stern on his conviction.
Prisoner of war but I still want more on restriction. My life
paradigm is paradox, but not a contradiction.

If you take care, don't miss this, I know you will witness this
message of wishes with intellectual fitness.
What's this surprise you see with gleaming eyes? We must keep
in mind: the mind, we clearly cannot deny.
We think therefore we are: all for one together and forever one
for all; need never feel alone at all.
All the best has come around so don't you frown and break down.
No more tears or sneers for the bore of poor years.

Because it's easy to get high on pity and pain when times are
tight; it's just a way to deal with strife.
Can I give you wisdom, light with these words I write? Fight and
never cease when peace is not in sight.
Quite astonished, must be honest, it's the sweetest life. Serenity
and security; you were the sweetest delight.
Love is pure, not deceitful. Can we see full reciprocation? Please
just be patient with my mental recitation.

Go down this path; it's only the start. Time to depart with new
possibility and purposeful positivity.
Quite positively I paid the full price, now I'm broke with this
unaccepted note. I owe delinquent bills of guilt, though with
time I paid with hope.

Better Judgment

I try to explicate: "I am he who must wait." Then better judgment
states: "We should have never been together."
Logical reason reinforcing reality dictates: "She is not here nor
remotely near; physically Izzy is gone forever."
However we weren't living a dream as I remember a theme
shared between that nothing could ever dissever...
The tether and pure pleasure of our beautifully bonded
heartstrings, beating in such sweet rhythm and measure.

But a true shrew tore us asunder, as she stooped to the damnedest
deceit: astute plunder. Became the Devil to equate.
I ate the bait from the snake. As she knew I couldn't consciously
contemplate, she hissed words in my face ensuring no escape.
Her shrewish snide smile of pure hate; her crudest sly guile to
date rape. So there is no debate to state: sick seduction was the
state, as is sex under dire duress.
I digress. In summary: I'm simply depressed by others' summary
constantly pressed, as only to a certain degree do I agree with
the rest.

I understand Izzy hates me, despises me and I make her sick in the
stomach. I know she finds my actions absolutely repugnant.
Though where else is there to go but down and plummet once
you've reached passion's precipice, sensation's summit?
I broke an oath of hope; lust was my love-sin. But hence from then
until the end, why cannot I see my friend; be her husband?
My soul is numb from it, so why is it her smile that I covet? And
why, oh why do I love it to always go against better judgment?

Because I can only be calm if I let go of the edge of insanity,
landing where my heart belongs: her arms.
I value Izzy above any other pleasure or charm, thus I will right
my wrongs and never again do her harm.

Time

Part I

I know nothing's ensured except death from this Earth, so one
time I inferred...
What pain and Hell would I incur if it happened to occur I didn't
have her?
Such emotion was spurred over such endearing words.
A simple fact for sure: she was mine and I remain always only
hers.

I like pure sunlight and I live for the allure of the night.
All because I find the sun and the moon to be quite a beautiful
sight.
But above all the beautiful colors together making white, her
smile makes me truly appreciate life.
My disposition is strife, because I severed our connection and she
is not my beautiful wife.

There is an empty hole deep down in my soul. I wish every day to
have simply done what she told:
"Be nice to me," sweetly said she. But I was always so degrading,
my words were so deadly.
She entered my world war and her love was disarming. She; my
adorable dear, my lovely darling.
It's not good enough to say, "I'm so very sorry." So I pray for a day
when we can again speak calmly.

My misery is simply that I messed up terribly. I told her: "I am
yours." And she said: "You better be!"
I'm not obsessive; when I sleep I feel her essence. My soul is
incessant. She makes my dreams quite pleasant.

Part II

Once in time, we were fine. Now with sight forgot: oh, how the
fight's been fought.
Time for my mind to stay on the grind. Hope I can find Most High
in the sky.
I'm a sinner but a simple guy; be perfect, I try. May our souls
revive because flesh does die.
What a blessed surprise to live life wise. Such a lesson disguised,
so open your mind and let me inside.

Trust it's worth the time. But what's left behind? It would be so
fine to treat you kind.
Love will shine giving sight to the blind. I am inclined to fight for
what is mine.
Deep in time, I remember inside that I tried and tried to
dismember my pride.
We were so high, we floated and flied. On wind and wings, we
propelled through high skies.

Time has made me a man so I silently endure the fact that to love
violently is not precisely pure.
Trust me so sure, I've been there before. When you get all you
want, don't ask for more.
I compare your hair a breeze, and your eyes a sunset. Heaven to
me when I breathed your breath.
Sweet as can be when I tasted your lips. I dream eternally of one
more sacred kiss.

One more time, we're making a killing now. Can you again be
mine? With no more forgetting how...
Love was taught. Listen to my mission now: although hope's lost,
it's purely love I'm sending out.

<u>Not That Way</u>

It's nearly 3 a.m. I can't stand but still I can't sleep.
Say a simple prayer, amen. It's in the hands of Izzy to set me free.
I've been alone for a long while. Even though I have known her
  smile.
All on my own is tribulation, a trial. I don't even know a number
  to dial.

And I'm not alright. At my bottom-base, I'm not ok.
It's not my fault things played that way, but I'll fight the fight and
  pray today.
But I'm not alright. Without her grace, I'm not so sane.
It's what she taught: behave that way. The wrong felt so right, it's
  safe to say.

Still, I'm not alright because I wish I felt no pain.
It's gone and lost, we paved the grave. The fear and the fright, we
  stay away.
Please know, I'm not alright. And know I'm not ok.
Sins have a cost, I paid my brain. Her beautiful sight! May I
  exclaim?

I truly adore, but she ran away. I wanted more, but she wouldn't
  stay.
To teach one more lesson, know this today: it's not as it seems;
  it's not that way.

REEVALUATION

I never had to reach to feel peace, for she was simply right there.
Though now I have to sleep just to dream her nightmare.
I'm too scared of love's bright glare and fully understanding that
life doesn't fight fair.
And although it keeps us in a tight snare, love is the one and only
light that life might bear.

I refuse to say those words, words I know she's heard thousands
of times before.
I resort to show her that above and beyond all time before, she
will be the one whom I dutifully adore.
I vow to somehow make good on my promise so I will secretly
love her until I have corrected all this...
Conundrum I created causing our debacle debated; a reckoning
too belated, bound by sin and hatred.

Although I may be a demon, I cannot quite comprehend the
reason why to see her face is a treason.
I can only reminisce about the past; mangled webs of memories
I trace. Still I remember her laugh, her face and being in her
better grace.
I love to remember but I hate my place in this circumstance of
fate for it's my life at stake.
Up to this date, is there medication we can take to make us
emotionally aware and mentally awake?

I don't need the females' sea of plenty of fish, however fresh.
Beyond all other details gleaned which are powerless, I desire
Elizabeth.
Despite distant dispositions; despite dismay. She is my night and
day; the sole reason I became this way.

My Memory

I remember that I wore you down, tore you down; I remember
that I dissected you, dismembered you.
I remember that I was so confused. I remember I told you that I
wanted to kill you.
I hated you, berated you and I didn't stay true. In growth, I
delayed you. Now I loathe that I betrayed you.
Thinking it through, please understand: my love-life's paradox is
that my hate was made because of you.

I remember my heart would beat terribly fast. When I tried to
slowly breathe, I would only gasp.
I remember our past. Who knew that between true lovers only
fear and hate would amass?
Do you remember that I got tongue-tied? That I could only feel
hate no matter how hard I tried?
Do you remember you said: "True love is a lie!" Do you remember
I said: "Some things will never die!"

I loved you so much that I hated what you were. For you were my
disease; love was a crippling feeling.
If we take life for granted, are we accused of stealing time we
waste while we blow through the ceiling?
I'm constantly metaphorically at your feet kneeling, trying my
hardest with sonnets to truly teach healing.
There is a mesmerizing memory with no compare: "Stare! We
look pretty together; we are quite the pair."

There is a troublesome truth now fully aware: I wanted to forever
stay right there underneath your hair.
Your hair, which I declared: "You are a pink mess!" Is now what I
love best, summing up all of my regrets.

ANGELS CRY

Part I

All we need is love to live. All you have to do is give: your soul,
heart and mind to find astonishment.

Increment by increment, I think it's time we implement a massive
soul climb and mind betterment.

We, you and I, are the relevant revenant, although the sign's
reading death and the thin line is evident.

We lost the Devil's bet. Goodbye, to Hell we're sent. No atone for
the throne so we can't even roam our settlement.

How can we correct the wrong to all right? Soldier march along,
belong to my fight.

Hold her in my arms so she won't cry tonight. We won't spite the
light so pure in our sight.

It's like saying, "I love you," when you know it's a lie. Ironic and
demonic to cry with dry eyes.

We cut ties, then love died down deep inside. Now I only hide, for
she spied my evil pride.

I was unwise but now my mind's in better states. A fire still
yearns, it burns; incinerates.

So starting right now, it's time to figure things out. Karma can
wander, then come creeping back around.

The last thing I wanted was to see her frown. But how could she
smile when I only beat her down?

Quiet for a while, my peace is finally found. Why should my angel
cry? Such a bittersweet sound.

The sorry situation's simple, so why does the pain still hurt? Like
the feeling of a mother bearing a still birth.

The Devil wears many faces; she is diverse. She rips and tears any
patience; efficacious as she dream-perverts.

Part II

Love's a soldier's state of mind: shoot to kill first. Death; I expect
we won't fulfill worth.

Seems like nothing at all could lift this ill curse. A great fall was
involved, still it could be worse.

Raunchy flirt with the Devil; felt hurt on a different level. View
vice versa, prefer to save the rebel.

Thoughts disheveled, though there's another point of view. So pretty in pink with her hair the same hue.

I dropped so many clues about how now I just can't conclude.
    Think about us and trust I paid my dues.
Veins borne blood; a real but painful truth. Insane with love; how
    she did disapprove.
Not scared to live alone; fear is fully known. Still I miss splendid
    pleasures like her soft, little moan.
I wonder about meaning; still living, hoping, dreaming: of eternal
    heartfire infinitely gleaming.

Angels cry when it's not enough to say, "Sorry." So it's, "Come
    back to me!" That I'm calling...
To my dearest, my realest, my love from above. Although in anger
    in parting, no need to cry my darling.
Angles cry when lovers speak lies; appalling in snide brawling. So
    it's no surprise we see the skies parting and falling.
Angels cry when folly always flies, larger lies starting; when upon
    the brink, we don't think, just sink, still stalling...

In this place, disgraced; life-state so daunting. Once again, it's no
    surprise sunrise divides the dark'ning.
Up to me, demons don't come crawling for my body's built quite
    strongly. For my sins of past, one last: "So sorry."

<u>She Said...</u>

Everything is a lie; this is not my life. Never have I allowed such pain and strife.

Junkie, addict, whore. Godless, helpless. Oh so sorry. I'm just so much a mess.

Everything's overdone; I have no control. Bones and skeleton; I'm no longer whole.

Someone save Izzy, for she'll end up like me. A whore for white nights with cocaine dreams.

Love me, leave me, it makes no sense. I'm falling faster now; fresh scars and gashes.

The love is a shell; I see clear carnage, I'm in fear. Everything's a shell. I wish you were here.

I wish I could say this straight to your face. I wish I weren't trapped in such a tragic place.

This is not a suicide note, nor a death list feeding from anger. Not writing a statement; I'm bleeding on paper.

I want it to rain, feel that real sensation. My mood reflects in loud cloud formations.

To know the future, all situations; to know the future, I have no patience.

If you would only stay, then I would always be with you. We became this way and we can work through this issue.

Love me, leave me, it makes no sense. We could roam together in self-conceived bliss.

She said: "Let's hold requiems for our dreams. Be bold, unclothe, roam alone in our dreams." Thus lucidly told what true love means.

A power pronoun: the lovely concept of "We." She said: "I wish to wake with you next to me."

INCREDIBLE

My dear, be incredible. Don't fear the Devil's pull. No hypothetical that life's methodical.

Sit quiet now and take it slow. It's just the way things are supposed to go.

Know how to grow so much stronger; weak no longer in this fight, toe to toe.

Unconditional love does not require quid pro quo. So show your undulating light shining to and fro.

Time's near, be incredible. Again, don't fear the Devil's pull. No longer pitiful; endear a better role.

Endure the damned in this listless, lifeless flow. Try this: row. Even if drowning in the undertow, have hope to save your soul.

No sneer, be incredible. Life is unforgivable but still quite critical. Like Alice who follows the rabid rabbit down the bottomless hole.

Let the master plan unfold. Live life; be bold. Light, behold! To again feel whole is the ultimate goal.

If I find you in a state feeling meager with degradation or eager in anticipation, believer just be patient.

Let's take back what they stole and stand the duration. A cold road alone but a chance to finally make it.

Birth a creation of souls in congregation. Worship love, not Satan, should be the focus of the population.

Mixed emotions of elation; integration of every high escalation in high frustration. Not mistaken, soul's taken. So me, put your faith in.

Don't only value your life when the end is in sight. I don't mean to excite, but to begin, what's right?

Don't live in regret when you see and feel death. Life's an incredible quest; in the end the soul's left.

Paradox

Part I

Noticing life's paradoxical politics is verily a must. In her
vermillion blood, I found love and trust.

I rode right on that bus, but with so much fuss that now I see I'm
on the cusp. Can you perceive such?

Life is a vicious ride so stay on the righteous side. Keep your eyes
on the prize, feel the emotion rise.

Fight for your natural right with all of your soul and might. Feels
like a hot time in a cold town tonight.

Telling bald-faced lies and barely half-truths, then sit and wonder
why all the drama ensues.

She's stuck in the pain; she can't remove her issues. She's past the
past events, but chooses not to move.

Her eyes like knives and razors too. To cut these lies, downright
impossible. The thin, weak line in sight, uncrossable.

She's bent on suicide. She says: "I'd rather die. Can't deal with
how I feel so this is: goodbye."

She holds hate until the last; still wrestles with it. She never lets
it pass and just be level with it, or let it be it.

But it's all over now; we see a brand new beginning. Still, in a
Catch-22, you can't count on us winning.

Sick and tired of sitting though still can't roam through the city.
Pray through all the pity. Satan come on and get me.

Everything connects, but not everything is connected. Ask for
more and get less, is a lesson; not deceptive.

Life is real. So tell me, why would you fake it? Love does feel. So
tell me, why would you hate it?

Mistake, just change it. The pain, just take it. The world has hatred
but I promise with love we'll make it.

Part II

I am a love believer; in business to enlighten fast minds. Enriching
mass souls; slightly daunting at times.

Though I know one of life's truths: the soul, we cannot lose. But
this issue's cutting tissues and a fact we cannot refuse is simply
this fact makes most confused.

I know life hurts at times, though maybe we heal with worthy
written lines.

With my plight, I see true lies as there is absolutely nothing more
to disguise.

I know that it's tenfold the time until I hold you again. Nine lives
to die but what lies within?
In the end like an eight ball; all that time to find that seven times
seven only equals forty-nine, too shy...
Of fifty mental backflips, filthy bad tricks; back to basics like
we're six. So rewrite the lines; revise five times.
With the other four iterations before, I couldn't rise from my
placement on the floor. Now I'm at your door, so say you want
more.

I remember our years were approximately three. I'm on a mental
mission so please follow me.
It takes two to make it all turn out alright. Though there's only
one heart; one blood. One love; one life.
And life treats us quite callous; bleeds hate and spite. But I'm sure
there's a balance: deep love over strife.
If you don't believe the truth that I perceive, just trust I don't
deceive. In me you find reprieve.

Life's a paradox, primal nature it seems. In love but love's lost,
though don't damn your dreams.
Give this time to set in and open your life perception. A soul-
saving lesson to suppress the depression.

RAGE

I want to tell the truth and put my mind to use. From old and wise
to all you reckless youth: come on and follow suit.
I hate myself; I debase myself. So ashamed in my brain and my
heart could melt.
Silently in my mind, I cry for help. Seemingly calm mind, inside
I scream, I yelp.
From the self-induced disease which I felt, I finally forgot my
dreams; on my knees I knelt.

I'm running through this life. Wait, walking. Wait, crawling.
I'd like to feel alright despite I'm falling. I'd love to pick a wife
tonight with no stalling.
Despite all my rage, I'm an intellectual sprite, I'm a spiritual sage.
I exert emotion in motion, thus I'm a literal mage.
Brands of love and my skin is engraved. I sin for blood; may one
day behave.

I hate the miserly, vicious cupidity. I hate stupidity; people
resisting listening.
I hate being me when my brain picks at me. I hate all I see; this
life is sickening.
I hate that I hate, but my mind's in misery. It's life or death at
stake so I act accordingly.
With simplicity I see that hate's a spoiled dream. I'm no longer
fake; true love and loyalty.

In my psychotic days, I was a soul full of rage. We met, made a bet:
love will last always.
I was a coward; threw away what I always craved. Knowledge is
power, though with faith to reclaim those lovely days, we're
saved.

Cocaine Dreams

Poised and alert, my postulating mind. I see a deep reverie down sands of time.

I try to find sense behind the events, though this life seems worthless; the path looks vicious.

Never say: "Never!" Except never detach. Simply endure the fact that cocaine does expend: Cost Over Cost Again In No End.

The appeal of the steal, the feel of the deal. Real cost over cost again in no end. There is no end to the cost within.

It's freezing and feels cold inside as the plan was premeditated. Lousy lies, demise; hope disintegrated.

We feel most alive when life is nearly completely separated. No surprise that all shall be wise. So learn, appreciate it.

The Devil does don a devious dress to disguise the depth of death and deception in her designs, holes in her lies, horror in her eyes.

Rush to fix that itch for the Bitch because you find white fine. Feel that itch rush quick; twist, spine grind.

Ten lines are chilling a weak coward. There's a man who wears a cloak, gleaming with power.

He lurks like the Reaper deep into the night with eyes beneath a heavy black hood to hide his fright.

Go now, run! You have to run ever faster. Running in the mind from your tragic disaster.

But you won't escape the Devil for Bitch awards no sleep. Forever flowing backward, adrift a sea of grief.

Amidst the mist so dense and darkness I see raw reality: at the very least the Beast is really me.

You're all alone but you still hear screams. Our sentence is Hell with no appeal to redeem if we fiend for false hope and cocaine dreams.

<u>We Know</u>

Part I

To begin: it's no surprise that life is quite a bumpy ride, but I see
your eyes show hope that all will be all right.

Are we alright or all wrong inside? Most of the mentally strong
can't even decide.

We're not abusive, no excuses, we just get high to get by. But the
actual truth is: that's just a flyby lie.

It's not hard to explain that life's a do or die game. We try hard to
attain, thus from vice we should refrain.

We swear: we know about dreams and nightmares. We know
precious things, not everyone gets theirs.

We know the depth of despair and heavy burdens to bear. We
know perpetual pain, hurting and energy drained.

We know blame and shame in the brain; we felt the same. For
peace, all we need is some support and relief.

Release us evil please, retrieve our natural liberties. We see, you
should agree: simply live and let be.

But what does life mean? How do we exist? Why does it seem
we're on someone's death list?

Could it all be a dream? Remember Supreme said this: "Repenting
is supreme, sins corrected."

Not deceptive so don't neglect this: time's depressive and oh so
hectic, but value's our vindication vested.

Perchance untie our hands; deny demonic demands. Devise some
better plans and see hope at a glance.

Whether called God, Allah or span spiritual spectrum to Hashem
or Jah. We seek to reach peace, can you perceive that far?

We know who we are; we shine bright as a star. Truth is our water
and bread. If it's lies we'd surely starve.

Part II

Carve a message set in the stone's slope for the wisdom to cope.
To know: you're not alone when you have hope...

Somehow something up high with eyes is also by your side. Quite
snide to have pride; virtue to put it aside.

Decide now is the time to strike and fight tonight. Because the
battle's arrived, now feel your heart rate rise.

Truth we'll find a suitable time to end our strife and plight as the dreams unseen have now come to light.

We know birds of certain feathers do flock together. We know
words with certain letters to bond whomever.
We know we're not alone, some love is forever. We know pressure's
on for the worst, but bet it's better.
Come out, come gather 'round, no use in hiding. Stay calm, don't
rough around, no use in fighting.
I'm bound to make your day a little more exciting. Together, keep
trying. Let there be no more dividing.

Calm weather, it's better to be true when deciding: when and
where to stay straight through a life that's winding.
Because reality and truth are often non-coinciding, when finding
time's not nigh however you know the timing.
Paths not only cross, mostly they are colliding. Though mostly
into hate, can we stay love-abiding?
Pray through despair; take care while providing. Declare mental
binding and share soul intertwining.

The timing of our plight; one-way journey through this life. Span
spectacular sensual spectrum from left to right.
We'll glisten in sunlight; see sweet things all night. With clear
minds bright and no need for fright.

Part III

In a time now a long time ago, there was a child that used to play
and every day a new roll.
Grew up learning ways at every appropriate stage. Now plays the
part of a being in-tune with the heart.
One step at a time, he learned to walk the beat. Then repeat,
repeat the process to gain all the knowledge.
To only be honest, must live life with the promise: to be supreme,
as to be highly astonishing.

Started following the right path at last to see the last destruction
of mental corruption.
The future is coming so forget the past. Breathe with ease and
don't gasp for dark memories.
We know demon entities can't destroy our natural liberties. It's
the exact epitome of excellent abilities; the meaning of the
little things.
Life's redeemed; not a fiend for false high. "Vengeance is mine!"

Happens to be the policy of Most High.

Accordingly acting; no more hate when reacting. Subtracting the
pain and re-waking the brain.
Learned all people are equal though no lives are the same. But the
fact remains most strive on past pains.
And for that fact the child's grown with peace that feels like home.
Truth shone; not deceitfully known...
It's the test of life to reach the crest of life. Know it's worth and
within all your might, so begin the fight...

Through this Hell we call Earth. You could tell what your worth.
We know, we feel, we see our souls rebirth.
Please repeat piece by piece, but only with peace. If you have
wide eyes, no cries. We know to die, re-rise.

Adalay Sunrise

My mesmerized mind is broadcasting in the blind; my only
leverage for sending a meaningful message.
We seldom select the perfect words at the perfect time. I try to
impress: some sights are too impressive.
I still recall that perfect day when I realized: together is the
perfect way; love's not perfect, but worth it.
So I smiled and mustered my strength, breathed deeply then did
say, "Darling, may I call you Adalay?"

For words bear meaning; my meaning being: my angel pristine
makes me feel like a real human being...
In a world with the waking, walking dreaming where nothing's
real, really we are only dreaming fleeting feelings.
The truth I am revealing is that I was humbled by her presence.
Through the nonsense, she made sense.
In my memory, a notion persists: emotion exists. Paradoxically,
metaphysical but still can be felt physically.

Adalay means: perfection without correction, beauty without
question and light leading my direction.
Upon reflection of her reception to my soul's situation, I was not
patient, thus the cessation of sensation.
Adalay is the love-Creator, thus I must belabor that my behavior
did waver in the presence of my Savior.
Made for my fingers; played identical dreamers. My love has
lingered as I am more than a simple believer.

I have known perfect peace fulfilled. Thus if she were ill, still I'd
remain right at her side for comfort as she died.
I would sit and watch while she dies, again a million times, to
wake up in a million lives with skies of an Adalay Sunrise.

No Words

I miss you more than words have power to express. I wonder if
this is the end or can we take a next step?
I feel absolutely blessed to have had the hours to lie beside you
chest to chest, for you were my best...
Friend, lover; above you there was no other. Our life-light warm
and bright, but hate caused a shudder.
It was your spell I was under so now those three trivial yet
powerful words, I shall never again mutter to another.

Introspectively I was constantly in a flutter. Emotionally, verbally;
I believe my words were what cut her.
In retrospect I regret my high mind was in the gutter. I expect it
was a test: simply to live and love her.
There's no phrase to properly pronounce the amount of my craze;
no ways to explain the bane of my days.
At nightfall I fumble, stumble through my mind-maze for my
ever-amounting shame still remains, stays.

I exist in a daze, thus it helps and pays to hold her in high praise.
I dwell in Hell with guilt of all our frays.
This primal position posited is passion, my primary purpose.
Peace and love lie deep beneath the surface.
I feel neurotically nervous and utterly worthless. There's no
sufficient verbiage, so she's never heard this.
Desire fueling our heartfire spurred this, stirred this. But no
more words we speak. Do we deserve this?

I am only a renaissance man made weak from her kiss with a
reconnaissance plan to repeat our first bliss.
To hold you once again is my real recompense. We together, with
no words. And all will still make sense.

GOODBYE

I swear unequivocally upon the Most High that I only intended to
give the concept of "We" a serious try.
I'm so sorry for my unacceptable actions and vicious lie. I am the
reason this happened and love did die.
Give me one more time to pry, to cry, to sigh. One more flight to
fly; one more night to hold you nigh.
I want to fly in your vanilla eyes but a question comes up: "Why?"
As such, this is my final: "Goodbye."

This is my final flash of memories past, remembering your arms'
grasp. I now bow alone; the finale at last.
The simple truth of my past is that I was riddled with confusion.
Now with pride belittled and mind disillusioned...
From my negatively habitual amusement, I saw the ruse end.
Time to tie up my love-life's last loose end.
I see truth but to you nothing's proven. I desire fire, though no
more fuel to spend. There is no win in our dire duel's end.

Lest my love should be forgotten; lest my soul should turn rotten,
I shall reach up and out then go all-in.
Seems we've reached the pinnacle of thoughts and opinions
highly cynical. Was our love story so typical?
The words of my message are not subliminal, rather right in your
face to state quite poignant and pivotal...
I will no longer feel pitiful over a guilt so reprehensible, recurring
repeatedly in a state of bereavement; sickly cyclical.

You were the one in which time I did devote. In my eye you were
my wife; would've been fine to elope.
So I hope you find this note referencing us and wrote for scope:
"Goodbye my natural high." End quote.

Untitled #13

*My life plays in monochrome slides, cast out between his comings and goings. An
  entire life of dependence and loyalty; an imagined slavery to his voice.*

*His kisses fuel this addiction; pressing like delicate fury and holding fast. He
  begs softly for this to all be real as we watch each other waste away.*

*This is poetry written in flesh, for each of us to consume. Doing our part to
  ensure life in the other.*

*These hearts are entangled, veins and capillaries. The simple bondage of our
  heartstrings.*

*The finality of his words make pain an entity of death. And draw me in close,
  deep into his embrace.*

*Listening to his voice as his lips move in rhythm with my heartbeat. The darkness
  and depth, the ratio of life the same as my own.*

*Listening to his words, his pain, is like looking in the mirror and tracking my
  own demise, his reflection is in fractures.*

Facets of his life, embedded in me; a museum of his history my body has become.

I surmise my demise has begun. My horrid envy, my torrid
jealousy; my pride got the best of me quite effectively to make
her defect from me, especially regretfully the death of "We…"

"I have looked the Devil in the eyes!" Some so speak. Well I flirted
in her eyes quite directly and deliberately, danced deviously
then I fornicated feverishly.

Trust that from the first faint, forever fleeting reflection or
realistic recollection of any kind…that recognition and brief
time between emerging from sleep and opening my eyes, your
memory is absolutely involuntary; you are the first thing on
my mind.

Thus that beautiful place and peace between awake and asleep;
that is the dimension within my heart and mind where you
shall forever reside. Truly in my weakest times, I feel you the
strongest inside.

Just a final-five. Five final days is equal to one hundred and
twenty thoughtful hours. Which also covers seven thousand,
two hundred measly minutes. Which is correspondingly
commensurate with four hundred, thirty-two thousand stupid
single seconds until she returned.

Therefore, there are multiple hundreds of millions of reasons undebated and truly discerned why I should have simply waited just under half a million miniscule moments, just yearned. But instead I degraded all of your trust I earned and negated all that we loved and learned.

Majority Rules

As 'They' speak their biases and prejudice on 'trusting' and 'familiar' ears, I am forced to sit, smile and stay silent. 'They' say: "Don't mind it! Just get it: just this!"

I am poetic justice. Even though my thoughts are reamed, my actions demeaned and 'They' say my motives are not esteemed, ironically I am the one in the majority.

But 'They' say: "It's all ok! We're only speaking hypothetically. And those people aren't in the scenery presently; those people are never behaving properly."

What 'They' say simply, the phonies in front of me, is invalid and invaluable to be. For 'They' failed and never valued to see: 'They' are the failures, instead of me.

The most grotesque mistake is to progress with false-faith and blind-hate, boast your weak-minded state and host debate that you're righteous, when you're fake.

'They' judge so easily and callously. Though the sickening irony is that 'They' are the ones acting wickedly and 'They' know nothing of pure truth and honesty.

I need peace for my mind. Thus, what is the purpose of this gift of mine? Why is it also a curse and constantly causes crimes? I shall attempt to reply to my own inquiry line: I actually attempt to acquire the Pure Truth that's behind, be beautiful and Devine.

I must dig, crawl and meander metaphysical mediums in the blind to find the land of infinite sunshine, where there is no more ugliness or grime, where being is being regardless of physical time, where hate is balanced and burden beautifully benign.

There is absolutely no restriction; we have every natural authority, autonomy and jurisdiction to be enlightened and uplifted in our perspectives, acceptance and directives. All previous terms in terms of the entire human collective.

What follows in turn are the Majority of One Rules to learn. Rule number one: Never let anyone disrespect you! So long as disrespect was never given directly from you. Rule number two: With pure hypocrites or those who lack common sense, never attempt to argue.

Truthfully, rule three: Remember every day of the week, never get tongue-tied or unable to rationally speak. What's important even more is rule number four: Don't debase your own dignity and pitch a fit in the floor. Still more, rule five I adore: Calm down; don't rant and roar.

As for rule six: Never simply 'spit.' Always have meaning and purpose in your conversation per the situation. And even in trepidation or intimidation, stay pleasant with rule seven: Don't hate! Truly appreciate! And last but not least is rule eight: Never be abusive or offensive! Be "The Great..."

Remember that we can make everyone feel so great by talking calmly, empathetically and rationally to handle any issue at stake, and we can improve other's quality of life, perceptions and opinions by being honest, not fake.

Traveling this intellectual, spiritual journey we all must take, follow the one that guides and leads all human beings by treating them as eternal ends and never as material means. But 'They' want me to fail, have bad timing and ensure that none of us succeeds. A fact highly obscene, overtly seen.

The Weaver

I used to be small; a short, small statured boy. But I still loved life;
all that mattered was enjoyed. But hate destroyed my poise
and coy; learning that love is a joy but not a toy.

Of the work I now employ, I struggle and I tire. So I retire from
playing with an eternal heartfire and skirting an infernal love-
hate tripwire, mired in my entire desire.

While all the while still not having seen a single dream come to
be the reality of the scene; only the guile of what seems to be
a genuine gleam.

There could be so much love and levity if only we were truly
inspired. I speak in entirety that which is verity and dire.
Unequivocally no liar; naturalistically a squire.

I inquire; I seek. For some form of release from my deep sleep.
Something to work for to keep. Something to fight for and not
retreat. It is pure passion I seek.

I have experienced entrancing entrapment. Lust was the
mistaken habit and love I did lack it. Happiness was forsaken
and hope was absent.

Everyone stood stupidly still, then all double-took one another in
a feculent fashion. Wondering: 'Will we ever uncover just what
the Hell happened?'

Though it only goes to show: now you know it was simply growth
which was stunted and flattened. Living fantasy, we have seen,
leaves dreams unraveled, unfastened.

But you can never know the price of inaction. And you cannot
feed on lies for any ration. Or else you will lie in misery and
mockery and see truth as infraction.

In truth, I am a has-been; as in: I had...I had so much. But now I
am heart-less, drowning in a hole of darkness of which I did
live to dig. Neglect respect and love is impossible to give.

Thus I did a quick ad lib; an improvisation of the mind to pose an
interrogation of what's behind and possibly find a qualification
of this divine sensation in my spine.

To define those whimsical yet critical words which were heard: I
do love you. Ensured as the fact eminently endured: death is
assured but our souls left undisturbed.

I am perturbed and immured by the knowledge incurred: you are
that which I will never deserve. With you so near, I remember

feeling as free as a bird; in truth my dear, you felt as natural as the cat purred.

I wanted to forever be hers; to share her food and bed, but only dread I fed. Though now the boy is dead; became a man instead: the mad magician, the cunning conjuror, the great weaver of webs.

Acknowledgments

Special Thanks To:

Conrad Jones for teaching me respect and perseverance as my Karate Sensei. Student Creed #1: "I will develop self-discipline in order to bring out the best in myself and others."

Parker Cason for being one of my best friends regardless of where we are located.

Cynthia Curtis for the positive motivation given as a substitute teacher at Brentwood Middle School.

C.C. Carter for being one of my best friends, the memorable times we've shared and more adventures to come.

Dr. David Brown for introducing me to logical inquiry and rational debate as a professor at Northern Virginia Community College.

Dr. Walter Hopp for assistance in coalescing my collegiate knowledge and providing mentorship and guidance as a professor at Boston University.

Kenny Kelly for being a true friend despite differences of upbringing and teaching me never to forget to use rationality and my natural abilities.

Levi Chatinover for being one of my best friends, every conversation we've ever had and all future meeting-of-the-minds.

Dustin Gleason for being one of my best friends and teaching me the mentality of forward movement in life as well as mental and emotional growth.

The Family of Melvin D. Law, Sr. & Dorothy Law for the unconditional love and support given throughout my life.

The Family of Robert W. Carr, Sr. & Mary Catherine Chambers

for all the continued love and guiding me to succeed through all situations.

Brenda Louise Carr for simply being my mother, prioritizing her family and children before herself and all the love she gives to everyone.

Extra Special Thanks To:

Jessica W. for saying exactly what I needed to know without even really knowing who I am, as a classmate at Boston University. I only knew her in one class but was Facebook friends with her long enough to receive an important lesson. I hope the truth is conveyed to you in this message as it has been shown to me:

Jessica Says:

We have one life to live. We are in this world and we make our own decisions. Free will presides over fate. We are insignificant until we create something for ourselves. Something that matters to us.

The subjectivity of the individual's experience can be overwhelmingly daunting and lonely, but the scarce encounters with empathy, clarity, beauty and truth make it seem almost worthwhile to endure.

Sometimes there are people, places, thoughts and emotions that enter our lives and make us contradict the way we may have convinced ourselves that our lives should be–or perhaps condemned to be–lived. These contradictions are rare. So rare that they have not yet succeeded in changing that feeling I have in the pit of my stomach that makes me perceive life the way that I do. But they are what keep me going. The moments when connection and meaning overrule coincidence and insignificance. The moments when we are reminded of how beautiful the world can be.

About The Author

Stephen was born in Chattanooga, Tennessee. He then lived in Boston, Massachusetts for two years before his family settled in Nashville, Tennessee, where he spent his grade school years. The frequent moves at an early age, from down South up to New England and back, allowed him to experience various different accents, cultures, nationalities, religions and personalities when he was young. An interesting anecdote about Stephen is that as a child, he found it hard to know exactly how to speak due to the words y'all and fixin' of the South, contrasted with the Bostonian dropping and addition of R's to certain words. This early education of differences between people has taught him to grow up with the mentality that everyone is equal, and that respect is reciprocal.

He holds a bachelor's degree in Philosophy from Boston University, an associate's degree in Computer Networking from ITT Technical Institute, and he obtained a master's degree in IT-Computer Security from Marymount University. Academic excellence is one of his core values, though he also has many hobbies, including writing poetry and screenplays, performing both onstage theatre and as a self-trained magician, as well as formulating a new philosophical perspective in the form of an existential theory.

Stephen currently resides in Northern Virginia. He lives each day by going with the natural flow. His life has to run like clockwork and music is the tick-tock of his clock. He wakes up, goes through the day, and falls asleep, to music. He states: "The sound of my own thoughts is sometimes light, fresh and happy. Other times, my mind sounds hard, raw and unpredictable. At base, my words are meant to be intellectual and spiritual, and my only goal is to communicate the truth of human life to the world in an effort to promote pure love."

Stephen can be reached at scarr@pradisia.com as well as through his Facebook author page and Instagram account.

9 789898 859478 16